Curse of the Were-Rabbit

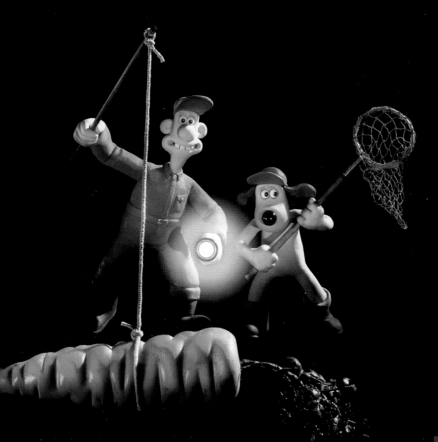

PUFFIN BOOKS

Published by the Penguin Group
Penguin Books Ltd, 80 Strand, London WC2R ORL, England
Penguin Group (USA) Inc., 375 Hudson Street, New York,
New York 10014, USA
Penguin Group (Canada), 90 Eglinton Avenue East, Suite 700, Toronto,
Ontario, Canada M4P 2Y3
(a division of Pearson Penguin Canada Inc.)
Penguin Ireland, 25 St Stephen's Green, Dublin 2, Ireland
(a division of Penguin Books Ltd)
Penguin Group (Australia), 250 Camberwell Road,
Camberwell, Victoria 3124, Australia
(a division of Pearson Australia Group Pty Ltd)
Penguin Books India Pvt Ltd, 11 Community Centre,
Panchsheel Park, New Delhi – 110 017, India
Penguin Group (NZ), cnr Airborne and Rosedale Roads,
Albany, Auckland 1310, New Zealand
(a division of Pearson New Zealand Ltd)
Penguin Books (South Africa) (Pty) Ltd, 24 Sturdee Avenue, Rosebank,
Johannesburg 2196, South Africa

Penguin Books Ltd, Registered Offices:
80 Strand, London WC2R ORL, England

www.penguin.com

First published 2005
1

Set in CheeseAndCrackers and WildAndCrazy
Made and printed in Italy by Printer Trento Srl
Colour Reproduction by Dot Gradations Ltd, UK

British Library Cataloguing in Publication Data
A CIP catalogue record for this book is available
from the British Library

ISBN 0-141-31889-9

GRAPHIC NOVEL

PUFFIN

Adapted from the screenplay
Screenplay by Mark Burton, Bob Baker,
Steve Box and Nick Park

Who's Who?

WALLACE
A lovable inventor full of hare-brained ideas, Wallace has a passion for cheese and tank tops.

GROMIT
Intelligent, courageous and sensitive, Gromit is forever saving Wallace from his madcap inventions.

LADY TOTTINGTON
Beautiful and wealthy, Lady Tottington is a vegetable lover and the hostess of the Giant Vegetable Competition.

VICTOR QUARTERMAINE
Proud and pompous, Victor adores hunting and wants to win Lady Tottington's hand in marriage.

VICAR
Mild-mannered and calm, the Vicar is easily traumatized especially when innocent prize vegetables are at risk.

PC MACKINTOSH
A voice of logic and reason, PC Mackintosh sees the Giant Vegetable Competition as causing nothing but trouble.

HUTCH
A cute and clever bunny, Hutch was cured of his love of vegetables by one of Wallace's weird inventions.

WERE-RABBIT
Eight-foot high and very hungry, the Were-rabbit is the terror of West Wallaby Street.

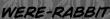

PC Mackintosh is on his midnight beat.

But all is not well. Something strange is lurking in the shadows . . .

SUDDENLY . . .

SNUFFLE

Something that darts into Mrs Mulch's garden . . .

GRUNT

RUSTLE

. . . and heads straight for her vegetable patch. But it unwittingly sets off a gnome alarm linked to the offices of Anti-pesto . . .

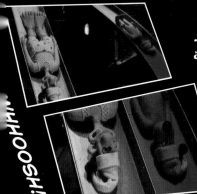

¡¡¡¡SOOHH!!

. . . also known as Wallace and Gromit, who have set a humane pest-control service to protect the town's vegetables. The Giant Vegetable Competition is just da away and Anti-pesto busier than ever.

PLOP!

SLURP!

The gnome alarm sets off a series of inventions that wake up Wallace and Gromit with a cup of tea, dresses them and deposits them into their waiting van. Anti-pesto ready for action!

ANTI-PESTO RUSH TO MRS MULCH'S GARDEN . . .

VRROOOMM

. . . AND IMMEDIATELY GET TO WORK.

Gromit manages to catch the struggling 'beast' in a large sack.

Cracking job, Gromit!

RUSTLE

BUT . . .

It turns out to be a little bunny!

Ooh, cute little fellow, ain't he? You'd never believe they could cause so much damage.

Oooh, me prize pumpkin! Me pride and joy! You've saved it, Anti-pesto!

Mrs Mulch's prize pumpkin is safe. All in a night's work for Anti-pesto!

The grateful townsfolk cheer as Wallace and Gromit head home.

Bless you, Anti-pesto! With you out there, the most important event of the year is safe!

THE FOLLOWING MORNING ...

Gromit rouses Wallace with his Get-U-Up device ...

BOING!

... but Wallace has put on a few extra pounds and gets stuck in the trap door!

I'm in the mood for fooood. Oof! Oh, er ... Gromit old pal ... Happened again! I'll need assistance!

FWAP

Gromit decides there's only one thing for it — a diet of vegetables! Far more healthy and less fattening than Wallace's favourite snack — a tasty slice of cheese.

Ah, still got me on the diet?

Oh, er . . . Gromit lad — how's that prize marrow of yours coming on? Must be a while since you measured it . . .

I need something a bit more cheesy . . .

But Wallace has got other ideas!

Gromit ignore: Wallace's cries as he finishes tending his prize marrow then goes inside . .

ARRRGGH!

. . . and releases Wallace from his mouse trap!

Oooh! Caught red-handed, eh, lad!

Wallace is just crackers about cheese. The only way for him to change his habits is with technology! This could be a chance to test his latest invention . . . The Mind-Manipulation-O-Matic!

It can replace bad thoughts with positive messages: 'Cheese bad . . . cheese bad!'

I haven't tested it yet, but . . . Whooohhh!

Wallace is interrupted by a phone call from Lady Tottington of Tottington Hall, looking for Anti-pesto's services.

I have the most terrible rabbit problem. The competition is only days away. You simply HAVE to do something . . .

9

Anti-pesto's van approaches the magnificent Tottington Hall.

Ho, ho, very classy!

OVER THE OTHER SIDE OF THE HALL ...

Lady Tottington already has another, less welcome visitor.

Victor! How lovely – and unexpected!

Heard you had a spot of rabbit bother ...

Victor, please, no! We can deal with this humanely ...

Victor Quartermaine plans to get rid of the pests his way – with a hunting rifle and his faithful hound, Philip.

It's off to bunny heaven for you!

10

MEANWHILE . . .

Anti-pesto get to grips with the bunny problem . . .

Burrowing bounders! They must be breeding like . . . well, rabbits!

But it's bigger than they bargained for!

Just as well Wallace has brought along another new invention . . . the Bun-Vac 6000 – capable of sucking up ravenous rabbits at 125 rpm (rabbits per minute).

But the Bun-Vac sucks more than just rabbits down the rabbit holes!

WHA~?!

SSLLUUURRPP

It whips off Victor's wig, followed by Victor himself!

GULP!

Victor can hardly keep his hair on.

This confounded contraption virtually suffocated me!

He retrieves the small, black, furry object from the Bun-Vac – but unfortunately it's the wrong one!

Victor?! Stop fooling around!

The ingenious Anti-pesto have completely dealt with my rabbit problem. Humanely!

Lady Tottington is delighted with Anti-pesto's services.

I'd be happy to let them roam free if it wasn't for the competition.

Gromit faces the formidable task of feeding all the rescued rabbits.

Their cellar is bursting with bunnies!

MUNCH MUNCH

MUNCH MUNCH

MUNCH MUNCH

But Wallace comes up with a brilliant brainwave.

The solution to all our storage problems!

MUNCH MUNCH

MUNCH MUNCH

Simply by connecting the Bun-Vac to the Mind-Manipulation-O-Matic we can brainwash the bunnies!

Hey presto! Rabbit rehabilitation!

15

HMMMMMMMMM

Veg bad –
veg bad –
veg bad.

. . . He accidentally knocks the
switch from suck to blow . . .

KLIK

Ooooh!
EEEEH!
Groooomit!

. . . and suddenly the Mind-Manipulation-
O-Matic is stuck in reverse.

QUICK –
SWITCH IT
OFF!

Gromit has no choice but to
SMASH his master's machine!

Get it off! Get it off me, lad!

KRAK

OUCH!

CRASH

Wallace pulls a petrified rabbit off his head
and offers it a carrot. The rabbit pushes
it away in disgust. Wallace is delighted
to see his plan has worked.

A reformed rabbit! We'll call him Hutch!

KLIK

Gromit tucks his prize marrow up for the night. Like the rest of the townsfolk, he can sleep easy.

RUSTLE

They know their vegetables will be safe . . .

. . . protected by the watchful eyes of Anti-pesto.

Sleep tight . . .

tik tok

BUT...

SNUFFLE

CRRUNCH

Later that night, a mysterious
creature is on the prowl . . .

MUNCH MUNCH

frail and the we
oh Lord ... let th
grow big and
strong ...

And as the vicar tends his
harvest table, he suddenly
realizes ...

... he is not alone!

N-no –
no! Mercy!

The townsfolk have gathered in the church among the upturned baskets and broken windows left by last night's intruder. And they are clearly not happy.

GRUMBLE

MUMBLE

GRUMBLE

Right! One at a time, if you please . . .

Someone . . . or someTHING . . . has plundered their gardens, ravaging their veg and wrecking Anti-pesto's alarms.

We pay good money for our crop protection!

Where were Anti-pesto when we needed 'em?

Only the vicar knows the truth . . .

A hideous creature has been sent to punish us all! The Were-rabbit!

GASP! Who will save us?

As if in answer, the church doors swing open to reveal Victor.

A Were-rabbit? Come, come now. What we are dealing with here is no supernatural rabbit!

It's a big fellow perhaps, but easily dealt with by a hunter!

But Lady Tottington thinks a more humane solution is required.

Guns will not be necessary. I believe the killing of fluffy creatures is never justified.

I say we give Anti-pesto a second chance! Mr Wallace?

Jealous of Lady Tottington's obvious affection for Wallace, Victor scoffs . . .

What! How on earth would those tiny-minded buffoons ever catch such a big rabbit?

All eyes turn to see what Wallace has to say . . .

Well . . . with a big trap!

By Jove – he's got it!

Aah,
LOVE, Gromit!
That's the
biggest trap
of all!

Wallace puts his
plan into action.
What better way
to lure a huge
rabbit-beast than
with a huge lady
rabbit . . .

. . . who just
happens to have
Gromit pulling
her strings.

Come on,
Gromit! A bit more –
y'know – 'alluring' . . .
Ho, ho, ho – very
cheeky!

Wallace gets so carried away that he doesn't see a low bridge ahead, which knocks the lady rabbit off the top of the van.

Blast! Stick around, lad. Should fix back on quite easily . . .

Gromit waits in the van as Wallace goes off to find the lady rabbit. But as the minutes pass, things start to seem strangely quiet.

Gromit tries to calm his nerves with a spot of knitting when something catches his eye.

*tik tek tik tek
tik tek tik tek*

Gromit realizes the van is parked outside a greengrocer's – and thinks he can hear strange noises coming from inside!

KRAK

CLICK

Suddenly, something smashes through the shop window and bounds down the street.

Gromit launches the van's Auto Lasso and finds himself dragged along by a powerful figure.

CRASH!

THUMP!

The creature heads for the back gardens and starts burrowing underground.

RRWMMBLL

The van is quickly dragged underground, and there is nothing Gromit can do to resist!

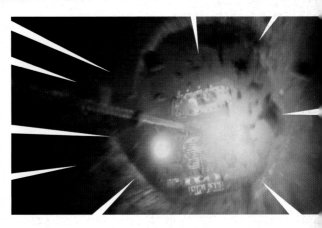

The van finally
emerges from
the mud. The
rope has
snapped and
the beast is
gone.

Oddly, the
burrow ends
right outside
Wallace's
house. Gromit
limps inside.

Where did
you get to, lad?
I thought we were
supposed to be
a team?!

But Wallace's
words fall on
deaf ears, as
Gromit spots a
trail of giant
rabbit
footprints
leading
towards the
cellar door.

Gromit nervously makes his way down the stairs, where he discovers that Hutch has broken out of his cage.

Wallace soon puts two and two together.

Ooh, Gromit! Hutch is the beast! The lunar panels! When the moon appears, he undergoes a hideous transformation . . .

OK so we've CREATED a veg-ravaging rabbit monster . . . but we've also CAPTURED it – like I promised Lady Tottington.

Wallace rushes off to tell Lady Tottington, leaving Gromit to build an escape-proof cage for Hutch.

BLAM BLAM BLAM

BA-DOOM

CLUNK

Satisfied with a job well done, Gromit leaves the cellar only to make another shocking discovery. The rabbit prints lead PAST the cellar door . . .

. . . and up the stairs to Wallace's bedroom! Could it be true? Could Wallace be the Were-rabbit?

The moon is already rising as Gromit rushes to Tottington Hall.

With the beast in captivity, the competition can go ahead as planned! You've saved the day!

Oh, it was nothing, Your Ladyship!

Oooh!

A grateful Lady Tottington invites Wallace up to her rooftop conservatory to look at her vegetables.

Peering through the glass, Gromit realizes he must get Wallace home before the transformation begins. He aims an asparagus spear at the sprinkler system . . .

FWISSSH

Success! Wallace is drenched and has to leave in a hurry.

Wallace is not amused.

As the sun sets they hit an unexpected diversion and head deep into a darkening wood.

I don't know what that was about, Gromit, but it certainly wasn't funny or clever!

AAARGH!!

A fallen tree blocks their way. As Wallace gets out to take a look, he realizes he has been caught in Victor's trap!

As the moon shines down, Victor threatens Wallace . . .

But Wallace ISN'T scared . . .

NOOOoo!

HHUURR!

RRRRIP

Victor looks on in horror as the transformation begins!

HOOOOOOWWLL

Gromit watches in disbelief as his master bounds into the woods. Already a plan has begun to form in Victor's mind.

So the vicar was right after all – there IS a Were-rabbit!

Victor hammers on the vicarage door.

I want to talk to you – about the beast!

The vicar lets Victor in and shows him a book . . .

THE OBSERVERS BOOK OF MONSTERS
BY CLAUDE SAVAGELY

Everything you need to know is in this book. To kill such a creature would require nerves of steel and . . .

. . . a bullet of pure gold!

Victor grabs three gold bullets from the vicar's hands and strides out into the night.

So, how's our rabbit monster? Hope you're keeping an eye on him!

What's up, dog? You look as if you've seen a ghost!

Gromit tries to break the news to Wallace, but he refuses to believe the evidence of his own ears.

The very idea that he could be turning into the Were-rabbit is ridiculous! Almost as ridiculous . . .

What? No! You think I'm the . . .! Aaargh!

. . . as the idea that Hutch could be turning into Wallace!

Cheeeeese. That's just grand! I do like a bit of Gorgonzola!

They spend all day trying to fix the Mind-Manipulation-O-Matic . . .

Now where does this part go?

. . . but Wallace is beginning to despair.

Oh, its hopeless . . . hopeless! Me mind's just a rabbitty-mush. I'll never fix the flippin' thing . . .

I don't wanna be a giant rabbit, Gromit!

41

Their work is interrupted by a knock at the door!

KNOCK KNOCK

You have no idea where this poor creature is!

It's Lady Tottington, who has heard that the 'beast' is still free to attack the Giant Vegetable Competition.

You've given me no option but to let Victor shoot the poor thing . . .

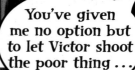

Shoot it?

Wallace starts to feel his ears twitching under his hat. The moon is rising . . .

It was a difficult decision, Wallace – I've recently developed feelings for you . . .

42

Wallace's transformation is coming on fast!

He slams the door in Lady Tottington's face, leaving her heart-broken.

Feelings? Oh 'ell, never mind. Thanks for coming, bye!

But Gromit spies Victor outside, just as Philip hands him his gun ...

Gromit must act fast to save his master! He puts on the lady-rabbit suit to lure the now-transformed Wallace out of the house.

Just in time!
Philip smashes
through the
front door . . .

. . . while
Gromit leads
the Were-
rabbit away on
a handy space
hopper.

BOINNGG!　　　　　*SPRINNGG*

Victor aims
his gun as
the pair
bounce away
over gardens
fences and
gates . . .

... but his first golden bullet misses its mark and hits Gromit's rabbit suit.

KRAK

Your loyalty is moving, unlike you!

The Were-rabbit gets away! But a furious Victor discovers Gromit hiding, and locks him in one of Anti-pesto's escape-proof cages!

Gromit manages to grab a trowel and throws it at a nearby gnome alarm ...

BEEP!
BEEP!
BEEP!

Smashing Wensleydale!

¡WHSOOHHM

... setting off the Get-U-Up, which flings Hutch out of bed, down the chute and ...

FWAP

PLOP! SLURP!

... into the van, which reverses through the garage wall, smashing Gromit's cage.

VRROOOMM

CRASH

46

Free at last, Gromit decides he must sacrifice his precious prize marrow . . .

. . . so they load it into the van, and hurtle off to save Wallace!

The Giant Vegetable Competition is underway. The townsfolk are relieved to hear that Victor has shot the 'beast' and saved their veg.

Ey look, everyone – it's Victor! Our hero!

Victor warns PC Mackintosh that the Were-rabbit is still on the loose ... forgetting about his megaphone!

Um, Constable... I don't want to panic anyone, but the beast isn't actually dead yet ...

THE BEAST ISN'T ACTUALLY DEAD YET?!

We must save our veg!

His chilling words echo around the fairground ... then panic breaks out!

QUIET! Let me handle this.

Victor wastes his second gold bullet firing into the air to silence the panic.

RRMMMBL

Suddenly, they hear a rumbling. The Were-rabbit is underground and heading their way!

Shoot it, Your Lordship! We're simple folk! Save us!

49

Victor fires his last shot, but it misses as Gromit rides into view on his marrow, pulled along by Anti-pesto's van!

Graaahh!

The Were-rabbit takes the bait and Gromit leads it towards the cheese tent . . . and safety!

SCRREEEEEEEEECH
THUD

No, Victor, what are you doing? That's m Golden Carrot Award!

Desperate for more gold bullets, Victor spies an old blunderbuss on one of the stalls, and makes a grab for Lady Tottington's Golden Carrot Award.

Give it to me, you . . .

Got it! Aha!

Hearing Lady Tottington's cries of distress, the Were-rabbit turns back towards the crowd, flinging Victor into the candyfloss machine.

Guuurrh ...

The Were-rabbit grabs Lady Tottington and runs for it, pursued by an angry mob.

Oooohhhh, gosh! Put me down at once, you great big hairy thing, you!

It climb
rooftop
where i
familiar
which I
Totting
instantl
recogni

Wallace? Whatever have you done to yourself?

Stand asi commission rid you c and that' I intend

Pesto? You knew all along! You're the real monster around here!

Vic
pu
Tot
aw
off
We

Run

Gromit has seen his master's plight and borrows a toy plane from a fairground ride. Gaining height and speed on the helter-skelter, he takes to the air . . .

VRRRROOOOOOOOOMMM

But Philip is in hot pursuit!

NEEEEEEEYYOOOOOOWWWW

Gromit spots Victor on the roof – he has the Were-rabbit cornered!

I've got you now, fur brain!

Skilfully turning, Gromit manages to lose Philip, whose plane plummets from the sky.

NEEEEEEEERRROOOOMM

Victor raises his gun towards the Were-rabbit and pulls the trigger – but in the nick of time Gromit flies into the line of fire and the bullet hits his plane!

BOOMM

AAAAARRRRGGHH

Wallace's heart still beats deep inside the Were-rabbit. It leaps after Gromit and grabs the dog to its furry chest to break his fall . . .

. . . as they plummet through the roof of the cheese tent!

Gromit is safe, but the Were-rabbit is out cold.

FWAP

=UFF=

Take that!

On the roof, Lady Tottington sneaks up behind Victor and whacks him over the head with her prize carrot.

Grrraaaahh!

Victor falls towards the cheese tent, landing on top of Anti-pesto's van.

Whaaaa–?

Gromit hears the mob of angry townsfolk approaching the tent . . .

. . as the van doors wing open to reveal he lady-rabbit suit n the back.

Gromit thinks quickly, zipping the stunned Victor into the suit and shoving him out of the tent. The perfect decoy!

ARRRGGH!

Led by Philip, the crowd chases Victor out of the fair and into the woods.

But inside the tent, the Were-rabbit has not moved since his fall.

Gromit turns to see Hutch . . .

Don't forget the crackers!

. . . who has sneakily been filling a plate with smelly cheese. Cheese – the perfect way to bring Wallace round! Gromit grabs the plate . . .

Stinking Bishop

. . . and waves it under the Were-rabbit's nose. Slowly, it begins to transform

Hmmmm? Cheeese?

Lady Tottington arrives and is delighted to see the 'Curse of the Were-rabbit' has been lifted.

Wallace!

As Wallace hastily grabs an old box to cover his modesty, Lady Tottington presents Gromit with a special prize . . .

The Golden Carrot Award – for your brave and splendid marrow!

GOLDEN CARROT

Wallace and Grom
finally piece the
Mind-Manipulatio
O-Matic back
together, restorin
Hutch's taste for
carrots . . . and
Wallace's taste for
cheese!

Job well
done, lad!

At last, everything is back
to normal . . . or is it?